1

Other Books by Author
Derek Slaton

Grindhouse Chronicles Series

1. Smoothen Silky: Demon Fighting Pimp

2. Midget with a Chainsaw

3. Curse of the Blue Diablo (Double Feature with Pestilence A-Go-Go)

4. Smoothen Silky vs The WereCougar

More information can be found at

www.GrindhouseChronicles.com

DEAD TEXAS: DAY ZERO

BY DEREK SLATON

© 2018

CHAPTER ONE

Tuesday, 9:47 A.M.

On a normal weekday morning, the newly renovated Austin police station would have been a bustle of officers and personnel. But on that day, it was sparsely populated, and half of the people who had managed to show up to their post were coughing up a storm.

Homeland Security Agent Harris was no exception.

"What do you mean you aren't coming in today? Do you..." he coughed into the phone, lungs rasping like hell. "You hear how I sound? And *I'm* here! I expect more out of my team. You can expect a reprimand in your file." He slammed the phone down in frustration before giving in to another coughing fit.

Captain Schultz stopped short as he walked by the office, taking in the sight of the middle aged agent trying to steady himself on his desk. He'd never seen the fit and sharp man look so sickly and broken.

"Are… are you okay, Sir?" the Captain asked, raising an eyebrow. "I can hear you from my office next door." He rested a hand on his considerable belly, figuring that if everyone was home sick there'd be lots of extra donuts in the break room.

"Yeah, I'll live," Harris replied once he caught his breath. "It's my fucking team. They're dropping like flies to whatever plague is going around this office."

"Is there anything I can get you?" Schultz scratched the back of his head at the sound of his co-worker's hoarse voice. "Coffee? Tea?"

"I need warm bodies, preferably from your SWAT team," Harris replied, sitting up straight. He abhorred looking weak and the way that Schultz was looking at him made him want to mop the floor with the doughy Captain. "Short-handed or not, we have to act on this intelligence."

"I'm sorry sir, but SWAT left twenty minutes ago," Schultz swallowed hard. "Apparently there is some major disturbance going on at the UT Campus."

"I don't care where you find them… just…" Harris wheezed and hacked, desperately trying to catch his breath and his words. "God-dammit. Our mission takes priority. I don't care where you pull them from, just find me some people capable of participating in a raid. Bring them to the briefing room in ten minutes."

"Yes sir, I'll see who I can round up." Schultz nodded and left.

Harris leaned back in his chair, closing his eyes and rubbing his temples in firm circles. Congestion in his chest, pressure in his head—regardless of being angry at his team this sickness was definitely unpleasant, to say the least.

His cell phone vibrated on the table and he picked it up without even looking at the caller ID. "This is Harris."

"We need a status update," an aged male voice demanded through the line. "Is your team ready to go?"

"Most of us," the Agent replied. "There is a nasty flu running through the PD here and nearly half my guys are down and out. I have the locals digging up people to fill out our ranks."

"I'm disappointed in the way you are managing your team, Special Agent Harris," the man on the other end said with a click of his tongue. "Don't make us regret giving you the promotion."

"We'll get the job done," Harris replied, injecting as much authority into his voice as possible. "I'll give you a status update after the raid."

"Very well then," the voice conceded. "Go get it done."

Harris ended the call and threw his phone on the desk in frustration, scrubbing his hands down his face. "I swear I'm making these assholes walk back to DC after this is over."

CHAPTER TWO

Tuesday, 10:02 A.M.

Agent Harris made his way to the briefing room, the lurch of his equilibrium reminding him with every step that he was unwell. It was getting worse; he felt like he was being eaten alive from the lungs out.

"Agent Harris!" Schultz called from down the hall, and the Special Agent turned towards the Captain with two people in tow. "Here are the officers you requested."

Harris set his tired gaze on the thirty-something Latino man with the hard eyes and the young looking redheaded woman with the small but athletic frame.

"Two people?" He squeezed the bridge of his nose momentarily, scrunching his eyes shut. When he released them, he ignored the officers, leveling his attention on Schultz. "That's all you could find me was two people?"

"I'm sorry Agent," Schultz said quickly, holding up a hand, "but the situation at UT still isn't under control, and half my officers are out sick today. So unless you want old overweight slowpokes like myself, this is what you're going to have to work with. I honestly wish I could do more." The determination in his face made Harris sigh.

"Okay, I appreciate it Captain," he said, and turned to the two officers. "You two, sit in the back, pay attention, and see me as soon as the briefing is over for your orders, you got it?"

"Yes, Sir," they both answered in unison.

"Alright, let's go," Harris entered the room and immediately the six strike team members dissolved their milling about and took their seats. The two officers took the available back seats, feeling tiny in comparison to the burly strike team members.

Harris stepped up to the podium and picked up a remote control, dimming the lights and starting a slide presentation on the overhead projector.

"Okay men." He stifled a cough. "Here is what we have." He clicked to the first slide, which showed a middle aged white man in a lab coat. "This is Dr. Alexi Sokolov, AKA the Russian Plague. Russian national, worked in bio-research for the government since his recruitment right out of college, and an all around despicable human being. In 2012 he-" Harris broke off into a coughing fit, and one of the strike team members leaned forward with a bottle of water outstretched.

The Agent took it and nodded gratefully, taking a deep draught and setting it down on the podium. "Thank you," he replied gruffly. "Goddamn. Sorry, as I was saying. In 2012 he was assigned to the Assad regime to help them with their chemical weapons program. We were unsure of his specific task, but we heard varying stories about compact bioweapons that individuals could release while on the ground. Kind of like a plague suicide bomber.

"It's unknown exactly how successful he was since in 2014 his lab was struck in an airstrike, killing his wife and lab partner Irina. It was assumed that Dr. Sokolov was also killed in the blast, but his body was never recovered. It wasn't until 2015 that one of our sister agencies picked up his trail in some of the less desirable parts of Africa." He clicked to the next slide, showing the same man with severe burns to the side of his face.

The look in Sokolov's eyes was haunted and severe, as if he'd come out of the picture and tear them all apart with his bare hands. He had clearly been unstable, especially after all he'd been through.

"As you can see, the good doctor here was alive, but did come away from the airstrike with a souvenir," Harris continued, pausing on a wheeze and taking another quick

sip of water. "Over the next eigh-
teen months he was tied to half a
dozen chemical based attacks around
the globe. These rarely got news
coverage in this country because
they were in places very few people
here give a shit about. But those of
us paying attention were growing
more concerned as his attacks were
becoming more sophisticated.

"Then, in the spring of 2017,
he vanished. We didn't know if some
third world dictator killed him, im-
prisoned him, or if he was one his
own cooking up something large
scale. We knew he was upset over the
death of his wife, so we couldn't
rule out a strike on our homeland.
Which is why we were activated." He
clicked through to the next slide.

The image showed a crowd of
people in the stands of a football

game, everyone wearing Texas Long-
horn gear. In the center of the pho-
to was a man in jeans and a plaid
shirt with a severely burned face.

"Is that *here*?" the red haired
officer blurted, startling most of
the room. A blush crept up her
cheeks as the strike team turned to
look at her, more than one gaze of
annoyance at her outburst.

"Anyway..." Harris cleared his
throat, sounding like someone was
juggling wet marbles in his chest.
"Three days ago at the University of
Texas Longhorns football game, an
eagle eyes security guard spotted
him walking around the crowd. The
cameras outside of the stadium found
him buying a ticket from a scalper
and then walking the outer rim for
the entire first half.

"About halfway through the second quarter a security guard noticed he had passed his post five times already, always walking in the same direction, so he called it in. Cameras picked him up and followed him from there. At halftime he stood in line for a giant pretzel and walked around the crowded concourse one more time before exiting the building a couple of minutes after the third quarter started.

"The security team captured him getting into an Uber and driving off. Thankfully someone had the good sense to run his face through the system. Three hours later we were notified and dispatched-" Harris doubled over this time with his coughing, taking a few minutes to catch his breath and stand back up. "Again, my apologies," he wheezed, taking a drink and waving off the concerned faces of his team. "This shit is the worst.

"Once we had a positive ID we had the locals monitor the address where the Uber driver dropped him off. It's an old warehouse about ten miles outside of town. The building has been under constant watch since Saturday afternoon, and according to the records half a dozen men have entered in that time, with nobody leaving."

One of the strike team members raised his hand, the deep scar running down the back of his hand to his elbow glaring in the white glow of the projector.

"Yes, Jackson," Harris wheezed, motioning to the Agent.

"How confident are we that Dr. Sokolov is in there?" he asked, lowering his hand and sitting up straight. "And more importantly, why haven't we already gone in?"

"The Uber driver said he didn't see any vehicles when he dropped him off, and the stakeout team got there within a few hours to keep watch," Harris explained. "We are confident that he's still in there. As for the second part, after reviewing the footage it didn't appear as though anything was planted or released, so the working theory was that it was a dry run.

"Homecoming is next weekend, so it's going to be the largest crowd of the year. With that in mind we wanted to hold off for as long as possible to get as much of this cell as we could. Any other questions?" He brought a fist to his mouth to stifle another cough.

The redhead raised her hand in the back. "Yes, I have one," she piped up.

"Okay," Harris said, surprised that she had the courage to speak after her last embarrassing out-burst. "Everyone say hello to the two locals that will be helping out with the raid," he encouraged, but the strike team ignored her, looking unimpressed. "What is your question, ma'am?"

"Why is he here in Austin?" she inquired, voice level and firm. "And how did he even get into the country if he's on the most wanted list?"

"Good questions," Harris replied with a nod and a cough. "Our best guess is that he snuck into the country with the help of a coyote, and this is pretty much the largest congregation of people that is close to the border. I don't think he has any personal vendetta against the city of Austin, but this may be the only large target he can risk getting to." He looked around the room as he attempted to clear his throat again. "Okay, anything else?"

The redhead raised her hand again, prompting a glare from her partner. She shrugged her shoulders at him flippantly. "What? He asked."

"Okay mystery local officer, I'll give you one more," Harris motioned to her.

"If this really was a dry run, then why take an Uber back to the hideout?" she asked. "He's avoided capture for so many years, snuck into this country without detection, and he gets sloppy now? Just before an attack? It doesn't make sense."

Jackson spun around in his chair with a sneer. "Listen sweetheart." His voice dripped with condescension and she narrowed her eyes. "We know you're excited to be up here with the big boys, but you need to learn your place. And right now that's for you to shut the fuck up and let the grownups talk."

"That's enough, Jackson!" Harris barked, and then immediately regretted the strain on his throat. He hacked and then took another drink of water as the scarred man faced front again. "Officer, it's a great question but ultimately a moot point, because we are going in now. I want everyone geared up and ready to go in fifteen. Let's get it done."

He turned off the projector and the lights came back up. The strike team stood and bustled out of the room, the two officers standing off to the side and out of the way to await Harris ambling over to them. He leaned on the backs of one of the chairs, taking a deep shaky breath.

"What's your name, Officer?" Harris addressed the man, who stood at attention.

"Officer Antonio Cruz, Sir."

"Cruz, fantastic, what's your story?" Harris asked.

"Ex-marine, two years in Iraq, spent the last five years on Dallas SWAT before coming here," Cruz listed off his history.

"Why aren't you on the SWAT team here, Cruz?" Harris raised an eyebrow.

"I transferred in about three weeks ago and they felt I needed to go through some exercises with the team before being put into the field," he replied stiffly. "Supposed to be wrapped up next week."

"So you are highly trained and professional," Harris mused and cleared his throat, taking a sip of his water, emptying the bottle. "I like it. Report to Agent Jackson, he's the big asshole who doesn't take kindly to questions from rookies."

"Yes, Sir!" Cruz nodded in approval and turned on his heel, leaving the room like a bird taking flight.

"And that brings us to you, my inquisitive officer," Harris continued, turning to the redhead, who was standing casually with her arms crossed. "What's your name?"

"Lacy Sparks, Sir," she replied.

"Nice to meet you, Sparks," he said with a nod. "So tell me, what's your story? Why out of everyone in the building were you brought to me?"

"I spend three years on the prison Use of Force team," she began, but Harris put a hand up, clearing his throat.

"I'm sorry, I don't mean to interrupt, but *Use* of Force team?" he asked.

"Yeah, whenever an inmate was being a pouty little bitch and didn't want to come out of his cell for an inspection, I was on the team that would go in and remove him." Sparks shrugged as if it wasn't any big deal, but Harris raised an eyebrow.

"Impressive," he mused, and crossed over to the water cooler in the corner. "I can't imagine too many women have that job."

"I was the third woman in the history of the prison to have it," Sparks replied.

"Very good," Harris said as he refilled his water bottle. "Please continue."

"I decided I wanted more than the prison life, so I went to the academy, graduated third in my class before I became a hand to hand combat instructor there," she said. "Been at this precinct for a year and a half trying to get on the SWAT team, but it's a good ole boys club and breaking trough is tough to do. So to take out my frustrations I'm a wrestler and current middleweight title holder with the South Texas Wrestling promotion."

"Wrestler, huh?" Harris wheezed but smiled. "Okay, pop quiz. Who is the greatest of all time?"

"The correct answer is Ric Flair," Sparks replied without hesitation. "Unless of course you find yourself in the company of some old timers in Dallas, in which case the correct answer better include a Von Erich."

"That…" Harris stowed the bottle in his armpit and politely clapped his hands. "That is the correct answer. Intelligence plus self preservation. I think you are going to do well on my team I mean how can I go wrong with the women's champion of South Texas Wrestling?"

Sparks straightened a little bit and quietly added, "just champion, Sir."

He blinked at her in confusion.

"I won a three way Texas Death Match against the Dudek Brothers," she explained, and pulled up her sleeve to reveal a three inch scar on her upper arm. "It's how I got this."

"Ouch." Harris winced.

"Yeah, that cowbell is a bitch," she agreed. "But I won the match and claimed the belt for the third time."

"My apologies, Sparks." He put up his hands in surrender. "You are way more hardcore than I initially gave you credit for. Welcome to the team."

CHAPTER THREE

Tuesday, 11:02 A.M.

The strike team assembled a few hundred yards away from the warehouse, taking cover behind a line of trees to remain out of sight. Harris crouched and waved everyone around him, so they were in a loose squatting circle.

He wavered for a moment, face flushed with probable fever, but his gaze was still stern. "Okay," he began, "here's what we got. Two entrances, one at the north end and the other south. Jackson, your team is going to circle around and take the south entrance."

"Yes, Sir." Jackson cocked his assault rifle with a firm nod. "I'll make sure we clear them out."

"Calm down, cowboy," Harris said quickly, putting up a hand. "We need intel, because if Sparks was right and Saturday wasn't a dry run, then we need to know what we're up against. Shoot only if necessary, and aim to wound. I know you got thrust into this position because Murdoch is MIA today, but I need to know you can be level headed and do what needs to be done."

Jackson scowled, but reluctantly nodded his acceptance.

"Good." Harris coughed. "Okay, let's saddle up and get this done. Jackson, signal when you are in position." He waved the strike leader off, and Jackson moved with haste around the building, four of the other team members in tow, Cruz included. "Okay, I'm leading this charge. Harper, you are behind me,

Taylor is up next and Sparks is covering our six." Nods all around, and Harris turned to the redhead. "I know this is your first raid, but we're going to make it was easy on you as possible. Leave it to us to take the terrorists down. As we move forward it will be on you to secure them, provided they are alive. Can you handle that?"

"Yes Sir, whatever you need," Sparks nodded.

"Good enough for me," he replied, and three clicks sounded in his earpiece. "Okay, that's the signal from Jackson. We're a go."

He led his team across the open ground, encountering no resistance. They moved quickly and silently, and reached the door, pressed against the wall on either side. Harris gave a silent countdown before turning and flinging open the door.

He swallowed the thick mucous in his throat and ignored his gag reflex entirely, work mode taking over and bringing him to attention. He led them into a mid-sized storage area, with floor to ceiling shelving and wooden boxes strewn about. They moved forward slowly, about four feet apart at most, training their attention on the hidden areas of the shelves to make sure nobody was hiding.

The group froze at the sound of automatic gunfire muffled through the building.

"Contact! Contact!" Jackson cried through the earpiece, and Harris immediately motioned to Harper. Before they could move, the crackle of nearer gunfire echoed in the space and Taylor's head tore in half.

Harris grabbed Harper's arm, pulling him behind a crate as a bullet caught the strike member's shoulder. Sparks dove behind a stack of boxes across the room, peeking back out to make sure that Taylor was well and fully dead and didn't need assistance.

She spotted the gunman on the far end, continuing to unload a flurry of bullets through the air to keep the group pinned down. She ducked back behind the crates, looking to her superior who was doubled over in a violent coughing fit. Harper was trying desperately to stop the bleeding in his shoulder, but it didn't look good.

Harris finally took in a breath and caught Sparks' eye. She motioned for him to lay down covering fire and he nodded, fighting the wheezing in his chest as he thrust his arm over the top of the crate to shoot.

She immediately darted out from behind the crate, sliding underneath one of the bottom shelves. As she came out the other side she fired, catching the terrorist in the kneecap, forcing him to the ground. Before he could get back up she sprung to her feet and launched a flying knee strike to his face, rendering him unconscious.

She stood over him for a second to make sure he was fully out, and kicked his gun away. "Clear!" She called, and strode back over to her superior as Jackson gave the all clear over the earpiece.

"10-4, Jackson, we're clear too," Harris touched the earpiece and then switched frequencies. "Locals, we have the building secure. I need a couple medics at the north breach point and some uniforms to detain a suspect."

"You doing okay, Sir?" Sparks asked as she approached, brow furrowed in concern. **

"Doing just fine, thanks to you," Harris replied with a coughing groan. "That was one hell of an effort, Sparks. Once we get everything under control I'm going to have a nice long chat with the SWAT leader about the fact you haven't had a chance with him."

"Thank you, sir," she replied with a firm nod.

"Agent Harris, do you copy?" Jackson's voice came in through the earpiece.

"Harris here," the Agent slowly got to his feet. "What do you have, Jackson? Do you need a medic or backup?"

"We're fine, but we have something you need to see," Jackson replied, and Harris and Sparks shared a look of concern as officers entered the space, descending on Harper's bleeding form.

"Come on, let's go see what he wants," Harris motioned for the redhead to follow him, putting his fist to his lips to stifle another coughing fit. She held her gun at the ready as she tailed him, exiting the warehouse into an office area that had been devastated by a torrent of gunfire.

Harris wheezed a growl at the sight of lifeless bodies strewn in an ocean of blood splatter.

Jackson approached him. "Sir, you need to-"

"What the *fuck* happened in here, Jackson?!" Harris cut him off. "You had orders to use non-lethal force!"

"Well Sir, it's simple." The tall strike leader shrugged. "They had guns, we felt threatened, we removed the threat."

"Guess what?" Harris stepped forward, nose a hair's breadth from Jackson's. His hoarse voice didn't waver an inch. "Taylor got his fucking head blown off, and Harper caught a round to the shoulder, yet that girl right over there was able to follow orders and secure a live suspect. Are you telling me you can't do the job of a local fucking Officer?"

"Sir, you can reprimand me later," Jackson replied, pursing his lips and glaring at Sparks, who didn't give him the satisfaction of a reaction. "Right now you need to see this."

"Fine," Harris stepped down and cleared his throat. "What do you have?"

Jackson turned on his heel with a huff and led them down a row of desks into a large office. Along the far wall was series of maps, and a lone desk with a laptop. Next to it there was a plexiglass cell with a single person huddled in the corner.

Harris' breath caught in his throat, and he narrowed his eyes. Who was this prisoner? He reached out and tapped the glass, and the man sprung up and dove for him, smashing his face into it. Harris took a step back in shock at the sight of bloodshot unblinking eyes as the man creature gnawed at the glass as if trying to take a bite out of it.

"Oh my god, it's Sokolov," he said, noting the burns down the side of the creature's face. "What in god's name is wrong with him?"

"I have no idea Sir, but it gets worse," Jackson replied, and motioned to the desk. One of the maps on the wall was of the UT campus, with arrows charting a path through it and around the stadium. The open laptop had some medical jargon on the screen.

"Holy fuck, the attack may have already happened," Harris coughed, "we… we need to get this analyzed."

"I can take it over to our contact at UT," Jackson offered.

"That's no good." Harris shook his head. "SWAT has deployed there this morning for an undisclosed incident. Between that, the zombie doctor over there and this info we have to assume the bio attack has already been launched."

"So where do we take it, then?" Jackson asked.

"I have an idea," Sparks piped up, and both men turned to her.

"Okay Sparks," Harris said with a wave of his hand, "let's hear it."

"Texas State University in San Marcos," she replied. "It's about a forty five minute drive due south from here, about halfway to San Antonio. There is a lab run by Doctor Alvison. He's not going to be winning any major awards, but he's a solid researcher who has been at the school for the past couple of decades. At the very least he should be able to make sense of what's here so we know what we are up against."

"How in the hell do you know that?" Jackson narrowed his eyes.

"I went to undergrad there before joining the academy," Sparks replied, eyes much harder when she looked at him than at Harris. "I was an English major, but my final two years there I was one of the ambassadors for the school that would show potential freshmen what the school had to offer."

"Good enough for me," Harris wheezed. "We have to assume Austin has been hit and proceed from there. Jackson, take Sparks, Ross and Michaels. Get this info down to her contact. I'm going to stay here and interrogate the lone survivor."

Jackson pursed his lips as he stared down his nose at the redhead. "Yes, Sir," he said reluctantly. "Come on, Sparks, get the stuff and let's go."

"One more thing." Harris put up a hand. "I'm activating the hostile zone protocol, and will let D.C. know where you are going to be. Based on what Sokolov turned into I don't want to take any chances."

CHAPTER FOUR

Tuesday, 12:16 P.M.

The SUV tore down the I-35, lights flashing as Jackson wove in and out of traffic.

"Before we left, Agent Harris said he was activating the hostile zone protocol," Sparks broke the subdued silence by leaning forward in the backseat. "What is that?"

"Look sweetheart," Jackson replied, voice dripping with disdain, "the only reason you are here is to give me directions to this lab. You aren't here to ask questions."

"Whether you like it or not, I'm on this mission," she snapped. "So you can drop the attitude and give me some basic goddamn information."

"It's used as a failsafe," Agent Ross cut in, turning in his seat beside her to try to diffuse the situation. He was a dark haired man with kind eyes, and she relaxed a bit at his far more respectful tone. "When we have to go into hostile territory or an unknown situation, we activate this protocol. Once this happens there are several computer geeks back in D.C. that monitor all locally generated non-traditional communication from the area."

"Why, though?" Sparks raised an eyebrow. "What would that accomplish?"

"Traditional communications might be jammed or taken out entirely, so you may have to get creative to get a message out," Ross explained. "You might only have access to a ham radio for example, so if you put out a distress call the boys in D.C. will hear it."

"Gotcha." She nodded. "Good to know."

"Where the hell am I going, Sparks?" Jackson barked.

"Take exit 205, drive about half a mile and turn right," she instructed. "School will be straight ahead."

A tense silence fell over the vehicle as they drove the last leg of the trip. Jackson drove into the quad and parked beside the student union, eyes sweeping the area for any sign of people. There weren't even any other cars. It was a virtual ghost town.

"Where the hell *is* everyone?"
Agent Michaels asked absently.

Sparks opened her door. "There
was a massive bed bug outbreak at
the school last week, so they can-
celled classes and sent the resident
students away so they could fumigate
the dorms," she explained.

"That would have been fan-fuck-
ing-tastic information to have an
hour ago," Jackson snapped, turning
around in his seat to glare at her
as she hopped down to the asphalt.
"If the school is closed, then how
do you know this doctor is even going to be here?"

"He's a hermit who lives for
his work," she said. "Even without
students he's going to be hunkered
down in his lab doing research." She
slammed the door and the strike

leader growled, exiting the vehicle with the other agents.

"You'd just better hope he's here," he warned as he fell into step with her. "So where are we going?"

"Through the Student Union, third floor walkway and we're in the science building," Sparks instructed as she walked, short legs managing to keep a brisk pace.

They reached the front doors, but when Michaels reached out to pull it open they were locked. Jackson pushed him out of the way and rattled the handles in frustration.

"So now what?" His voice raised an octave and Sparks fought the urge to roll her eyes.

"Looks like we're going on a hike," she replied. "Just follow the

sidewalk around and it's the building directly behind this one."

The tall agent shook his head
in disgust. "Okay, let's go."

Tuesday, 12:38 P.M.

The foursome exited a dimly lit
stairwell into a long hallway, the
only illuminated lab at the very
end. There was no movement but at
least the lights were on.

"You'd better hope he's here,"
Jackson sneered. "If not, we're all
kinds of fucked if an attack has
happened."

Sparks ignored him and led them
down the hallway, stopping to knock
politely on the doorframe to the
lab. There were two young college
kids standing with their backs to

the door, and they jumped at the
sound, whipping around.

"You aren't supposed to be in
here!" The slight and taller one
with glasses said, though his high
pitch didn't really give off an air
of authority.

"We're here to see Dr.
Alvison," Sparks replied gently.

"Yeah?" The other kid, a short
and stout fun house mirror reflec-
tion of the first one, crossed his
arms. "And who are you exactly?"

Jackson growled and pushed his
way through the door. "We're from
the motherfucking U S of A government and we don't have time for your
bullshit," he fumed. "Now is Dr.
Alvison here or not?"

The kids blinked at him in fear
and shock, but before anyone moved
an older man appeared from the back

room. He was wearing a white lab coat and silver rimmed glasses and he snorted, wiping his nose clean before straightening to look at the agent, seemingly unimpressed.

"I'm Dr. Alvison," he said. "What can I do for you?"

"Doctor, we have a situation and need your help," Sparks spoke up, and walked over to him, taking his arm to help him sit in his desk chair.

"Very well," the old man replied. "What is it?"

Ross approached and set the laptop and documents on his desk, leaning over to motion to one of the folders. "We believe that there has been a bio-terrorist attack in Austin, and we need to know what we are dealing with," he explained.

Dr. Alvison took a moment to look over the first folder and then pursed his lips. "Okay, I'm going to need some time."

Jackson slammed his hand down on the counter behind them, startling the whole room. "We don't *have* time!" he snapped.

"Well," Dr. Alvison coughed. "Ugh, excuse me. Been under the weather for a couple of days now. Ted over there brought me this little gift on Sunday, didn't you Ted?"

"Hey, focus." Jackson snapped his fingers. "Can you decipher this or not?"

"Yes, I can," Dr. Alvison replied in a steely tone, staring the agent down with no sign of being intimidated. "But as I stated before, it's going to take some time. This isn't a football box score, this is complicated material. Could take me hours to figure out what this is."

"Fucking hell," Jackson grunted. "Ross, get on the line back to Agent Harris and give him an update."

Ross nodded and left the room to make his call, while Dr. Alvison swiveled in his chair to fully face Jackson.

"If you can run an errand for me, the process might be sped up considerably," the old man said.

"Great, what do you need?" Jackson rolled his eyes.

"Two of my research assistants, Ben and Ashley, went to Mike's Diner on the quad about half an hour ago for a late lunch," the Doctor replied. "If you can get them back here they can help me figure this out faster."

"Now we're talking," Jackson huffed, and turned to the redhead. "Sparks, go collect the young people so we can get this ball rolling."

"Why me?" she asked without thinking.

"Because I gave you a fucking order, that's why," Jackson hissed, stepping right up into her face. "You wanted to be a member of the team, well here you are, on the bottom rung of the ladder. So go get this done."

She bit her tongue, and as much as she wanted to comment about the way his breath on her made her skin crawl, she managed to hold back. "Yes, Sir."

"Jackson, I got nothing," Ross rushed back into the room.

"What the fuck do you mean, you got *nothing*?" Jackson snapped.

"Can't reach Harris." Ross shook his head. "I tried the police station dispatch and the Captain's direct line. Nothing all the way around."

Jackson's gaze turned from fuming to concerned. "Sparks, hurry," he urged. "This could be a real shit show in the making. And for the love of god, don't tell anyone what's going on. Last thing we need is a panic on our hands."

She nodded and practically flew down the hallway.

CHAPTER FIVE

Tuesday, 12:59 P.M.

Sparks jogged across the quad to Mike's Diner, red hair fluttering behind her in the afternoon breeze. She'd frequented the place a lot when she was an undergrad, being a staple of the campus.

She opened the door and almost clocked Mike Venture in the face who was standing right behind it.

"I'm sorry ma'am, but we're closing up for the day," he said in a tired voice. "My staff called in sick so it's just been me today. And frankly it's not worth staying open past lunch since nobody is on campus."

"Don't worry Mike," she said and flashed her badge. "I'm just here to collect a couple of people and we'll be on our way."

"Who are you arresting?" His eyes grew wide. "What did they do?"

"No, no, nothing like that." She put a hand up. "I'm looking for Ben and Ashley. Doctor Alvison sent me down here to collect them."

"Oh, okay, I gotcha," Mike replied with a sigh of relief. "They are the couple in the center booth there." He motioned and she nodded.

"Thanks, Mike," she said, and made her way towards them as he locked the door. The sight of the Mike's military themed decor to honor his Vietnam war days brought back a wave of nostalgia but she focused on casing the joint. There was a large bald man that looked to be in his late 30s wearing a black leather jacket at a table to the left, and two other inconspicuous looking men sitting by themselves along the far wall.

She stopped in front of the center table with a fit black man sporting a tight afro and a blonde girl that looked like she just walked out of a fashion magazine. They couldn't have been much older than 20.

"Are you Ben and Ashley?" she asked.

"Who wants to know?" Ben narrowed his eyes in suspicion.

"My name is Lacy Sparks and I'm with the Austin police department," the redhead explained and flashed her badge again. "Doctor Alvison sent me down here to retrieve you for a time sensitive project."

"Why in the world would he send a cop down here to get us?" Ben asked. "An Austin cop at that?"

"That… that's classified," Sparks said quietly, squaring her shoulders. "Come on, we really need to get going."

"Is this about all the sick people?" Ashley piped up, eyes curious.

"I… I don't know what you're talking about," Sparks bit her lip.

"Don't treat us like children, Ms. Sparks," the blonde girl straightened in her seat. "We both know what kind of research Dr. Alvison does, any my roommate is an intern at the hospital. She has been sending me updates on what's going on over there. Hundreds of people have checked in just today, all with

the same symptoms. That isn't normal."

Her voice was loud enough to
alert one of the male patrons from
the far wall. "Do you know anything
about the sickness going round?" He
called.

"I assure you, I don't know
anything." Sparks put a hand up.

"I took my wife to the hospital
six hours ago and the place was
packed," he continued, walking towards them. "They took her to the
back and the doctor isn't allowing
me to see her. Please, what do you
know?"

"Sir, I'm sorry but I can't
help you," Sparks replied, shaking
her head. "I don't know anything."
She was about to go on the defensive
as the man continued to move towards

her, but a banging on the front door made them all stop.

"We're closed!" Mike yelled from wiping tables, but the banging continued. "Goddammit I said we're closed!" He approached the door with a heavy sigh and unlocked it. "Are you deaf I said we're-"

As the door swung open a man shoved his way in, snarling and attached himself to Mike's throat. The diner owner tumbled backwards in shock, screaming as the rabid looking man tore at his flesh with his teeth.

Sparks drew her gun. "Put your hands up, now!" she screamed, and the grotesque man turned his attention on her like a bird hearing a noise. His whole face covered in blood from his ministrations, he leapt from Mike's lifeless body and darted towards her.

Sparks unloaded three bullets into her attacker but they didn't slow him down, and she ducked under his grasp and took him around the waist, flinging him up and over her head. He flew into a table and flopped over it like a rag doll, and she spun around to see him bounce right back up onto his feet.

The bald patron intercepted the attacker with a shoulder bash, and leapt on top of him once he hit the ground. He held the cannibal by the throat with one hand and an arm with the other, his prisoner's free arm flailing and smacking wetly against the leather jacket.

"Can one of you assholes help me out here?" The bald man grunted, and Ben ran over, skidding to a stop to hold down the free arm.

Sparks rushed over, staring down at the milky dead eyes on the creature's face. It looked like Sokolov. What was happening?

"Don't just stand there, kill this motherfucker!" The bald man barked.

"I put two in his chest and it didn't slow him down, so I'm open to suggestions!" Sparks snapped.

"Take his head off!" Ben cried. She aimed her gun but then thought better of it, holstering the weapon. "What are you doing?!" he wailed, and she turned to grab the heavy based sign next to one of the tables reading *This Section Closed*. She got a good grip on the neck and raised it to bash the creature's head in.

"STOP!" the other patron from the far wall screamed, standing with his hands out. "That's a human being! Don't kill him!"

"You! Shut the fuck up!" the bald guy demanded, and then looked up at Sparks. "You! Kill this motherfucker!" She didn't hesitate this time before bringing the sign down onto the creature's face. A few forceful blows and it stopped moving, and the trio relaxed.

The terrified patron ran straight out the door, and Sparks watched in horror as he got halfway across the quad before a pile of zombies took him down. One broke away from the feeding frenzy to tear at the open door.

"Get the door!" She screamed and dove forward, shoving it as hard as she could. The zombie hit the wood, applying just enough pressure that she couldn't get it closed, so Ben and Baldy threw their weight against it as well.

"Ben, look out!" Ashley shrieked as Mike's hand closed around Ben's foot. He stared down in frozen horror at the dead blood-soaked face of the man that had served him lunch so many long school days.

There was a sick squelch as Baldy brought his combat booted foot down on top of Mike's skull, twice in quick succession.

Ben swallowed hard as the hand let go. "Thanks, man." He rushed over to Ashley quickly, folding her into a tight hug.

"You." Sparks pointed at the man who'd been worried about his wife. "Go make sure the back door is secured and there isn't another way in here." She instructed, and he darted off before she turned to Baldy. "You okay?"

"Just fine, thank you," he drawled, but then clucked his tongue as she started to walk away. "So, are you ready to drop the act and tell us what the fuck these things are?"

Sparks sighed. "I don't know what they are, but I will tell you what I do know."

"Fair enough," he replied, crossing his arms expectantly.

"Earlier today, we raided a terrorist compound outside of Austin," Sparks began. "We took out what we thought was a cell that was prepping a bio-terror attack, but as we're finding out may have already launched it. We found one of these things at the hideout along with a lot of data, so we came here to see Dr. Alvison in the hopes he could decipher it and let us know what we're facing."

The banging on the windows and doors continued to escalate, and they looked around at each other.

"We should probably lay low, get away from their view," Baldy suggested.

"Not a bad idea," Sparks agreed, and led him back towards Ben, Ashley, and the patron that had secured the door. They hunkered down behind the food counter, out of sight. The bald man took off his leather jacket with a whoosh of breath, revealing some crudely drawn World War II era German military tattoos.

"What the hell, man?!" Ben's mouth fell open. "You're a fucking Nazi?"

"Relax kid," Baldy replied calmly. "They were necessary for me to survive some youthful transgressions, that's all."

"What does that even mean?" Ben snapped.

"It means he got ink in prison so he wouldn't get shanked in the meal line," Sparks piped up.

"Bullshit!" the dark skinned boy countered. "Man what do you have against minorities?"

"Really?" Baldy threw his hands up. "We just saw two people get eaten alive and we're currently surrounding by half a dozen zombies, and you want to know my thoughts on race relations?"

Ben crossed his arms. "Call it self preservation."

"All you need to do is ask yourself one question," the older man replied. "Given our current situation, would you rather have me standing here, or some pansy ass liberal that would want to go hug it out with them?"

"Um, I…" Ben stammered.

"He…" Sparks looked at the bald guy expectantly.

"Jeff," he offered.

"Jeff has a point," she continued. "Let's try to focus on the problem at hand and not create new ones."

"Ms. Sparks?" Ashley cut in, wringing her hands.

"Please, just call me Sparks."

"Okay, Sparks." The blonde nodded. "What's the plan?"

"We're going to lay low for a few minutes and hope they lose interest and move on," Sparks replied.

"And what's the plan when they *do* move on?" Jeff asked.

"We need to get to the science building," she told him. "My team is there with Dr. Alvison so we'll have some protection and can find out what we're dealing with. Unfortunately it's a long ass haul to the science building since the student union is locked."

"I have a key that can get us in," Ashley put in. "Dr. Alvison lent me his faculty key when we came out for lunch."

"That makes me feel a little better," Sparks admitted. "Running across the quad is a lot easier than trying to get all the way around the union. At least when we're inside we'll have some choke points where we can hold them off."

Jeff nodded. "That's sounds like as good a plan as any." He hopped up into a booth and stretched out his legs, taking up the entire seat in a pose of pure relaxation. The banging and groaning from outside intensified. "Guess we should get comfortable. Sounds like we might be awhile."

CHAPTER SIX

Tuesday, 6:22 P.M.

As the sun started to set, the banging slowly ceased, though upon peering through the windows the inhabitants of Mike's Diner could still see the zombies milling about.

"Fuck, they are up to ten," Sparks murmured as she squinted through the blinds, and turned back to face her impromptu crew. "I don't see our situation improving, so once the sun sets and we have a little bit of cover we need to make a run for it."

"That gives us what, about fifteen minutes to come up with a plan?" Jeff scoffed.

"I'm open to suggestions," Sparks retorted.

"What if we barrel through them?" Ben asked.

"Might work for us, but not some of the slower members of the group," Jeff replied, motioning to the diner patron who'd been worried about his wife. He hadn't said a word the entire time since he checked the back door, and they didn't know if he'd even run with them. "Unless of course you're okay sacrificing our boy over there."

"Man, come on." Ben sighed. "I wasn't suggesting that."

"Relax kid, I know," Jeff insisted. "The reality is though that most of us wouldn't make it if we tried your plan."

"Okay, so what's your big idea?" Ben crossed his arms.

The bald man smiled. "Let's give em the ole okey doke."

There was an awkward silence until Ben raised a hand. "Umm… what the hell is that?"

"You know," Jeff prompted, "from Dawn of the Dead?"

"Is that the one with the dad from Modern Family?" Ashley asked.

"Goddamn kids these days," Jeff muttered, scrubbing his hands down his face. "No respect for the classics." He sighed. "What it means is that we're going to create a distraction to clear our path. This place has a back loading door, right?"

"Yeah." Ben nodded. "In the kitchen. Leads directly out behind the building."

"So we pop our heads out there, make some noise and those zombies out there come and see what's up,"

Jeff said. "At the very least it should thin their numbers out some."

"Seems risky," Ben replied.

"Ben, anything we do at this point is going to be risky," Sparks piped up. "This seems like the best option."

"Okay, it's settled then," Jeff said with finality, rolling his shoulders. "Let's get loaded up." They started pulling some of the memorabilia from the walls, machetes and batons, anything that could be used as a weapon or to make noise.

Sparks took pause as the mute patron didn't move, curled up in the fetal position in a booth. "What's your name?" She asked gently.

"My- my name is Kyle," he whispered.

"Okay Kyle," Sparks said firmly. "I'm sure you heard but we're

77

going to make a run for it." She motioned to the front door with the baton she'd liberated from the wall.

"Nope." He shook his head violently in protest. "I'm just going to wait right here for the police to come."

"Kyle, I *am* the police," she said, leaning forward. "And I'm all that's coming to help. It isn't going to safe here once we open the front door."

"Nope, nuh-uh," he continued as if she hadn't said anything, "I'm staying here where it's safe."

Jeff walked up and flattened his hands down on the diner table, staring Kyle down. "Listen motherfucker, it's the end of the world and you got two choices. You can fight or you can lay down and die. If you'll notice wasting my goddamn time and endangering my life because you're a pussy isn't one of the choices. So what's it gonna be?"

Sparks blinked at the bald man's sudden harshness, but Kyle clenched his jaw and stood up from the booth.

"Okay," he said firmly. "I'll come."

Jeff winked at Sparks before leading the way to the back door.

"Okay guys, here we go," the redhead said. "Jeff and I will create a diversion. I want the three of you to wait by the front door. If this goes to plan we're going to be moving quick."

"We'll be ready," Ben assured her.

Sparks joined Jeff, gun drawn, and he raised his machete and put his hand on the door handle.

"Okay, on three," he said. "One. Two."

"Wait," she said.

"Don't puss out on me now." Jeff raised an eyebrow, and Sparks shot him a death glare that said *motherfucker please*.

"First off, if you ever had to pick up my balls, you'd throw your back out," she huffed, and he cracked a smile. "Secondly, I'm going to grab some pots and pans. Should go a long way towards making noise."

"And here I was thinking you'd just fire off a couple of rounds." He watched her rummage for a few thin pans with a skeptical look on his face.

"I only have twenty-six shots left, and I get the sense I

shouldn't be wasting them," she said as she rejoined him at the door.

"That's a valid point," he agreed, and then took the handle again firmly.

Sparks nodded. "Okay, zombie distraction, take two."

"Again, on three," he said. "One. Two. Three!" He flung the door open and they burst outside, scanning the vicinity for enemies. There were two zombies about fifty yards away who were feasting on a victim, and they shot to attention at the noise.

Sparks gave Jeff a nod and dove for the dumpster to the right of them, banging on it with the pots and pans like a death metal drummer. Screeches in the distance alerted them that zombies were headed their way, and she dropped the pans to dart back towards Jeff at the door.

He reeled back and slammed the machete into the top of a wayward zombie's head, stopping it dead in its tracks. Before he could wrench the blade free, Sparks landed a flying kick to the zombie's chest, dislodging the body from the weapon.

"Let's go!" She exclaimed, and tore back inside. Jeff slammed the door and locked it, banging on it a few more times for good measure. They barreled back through the diner to meet up with the rest of the group.

"There are still some out there," Ben said tersely, clutching his baton with white knuckles.

"We're gonna have to chance it," Jeff replied, peering at the three zombies milling about, still relatively close to the door.

Ben swallowed hard. "But…"

"Jeff is right," Sparks cut in. "This is our only chance. Here's the plan. When that door flies open, I want Ashley to run as fast as she can to the Student Union to get that door unlocked. Jeff and I will take the two on the right, Ben, you take the one on the left."

"Wh-what about me?" Kyle stammered, his big eyes watery.

"You can help Ben," Jeff said, and the student scowled at the skinhead, receiving only a smile in return.

"Okay." Sparks nodded. "Go!" She flung the door open, and Ashley sprinted straight ahead, a blur of blonde zipping across the quad. Jeff lunged to the right and in a powerful arc, beheaded his zombie quickly. Sparks bludgeoned hers in the head three times in succession before it stopped moving, just as Ben's zombie grabbed him by the arms.

"Goddammit man, help me!" he cried to Kyle, who was frozen in the doorway of the diner.

"I'm… I'm sorry!" He backed inside slowly, fear frozen on his face, and Ben let out a groan of frustration as he continued to wrestle with his snapping enemy.

"Duck!" Jeff screamed, and the student complied, leaning just out of the way so that the bald man could swing his machete into his opponent's face. "Let's go!" He screamed as the body fell, and he shoved Ben after Sparks.

"They're coming!" the redhead yelled, sprinting in the direction of the Student Union. A few zombies staggered from around the building and ambled after them. "Open the door!" Sparks demanded as they caught up to Ashley, the blonde fumbling with the key.

"The key isn't working!" she shrieked, and Ben looked fearfully behind them to see two zombies overtake the diner door. He swallowed at the thought of Kyle's demise, and shook his head to try to focus on the task at hand.

"Well, you've got about ten seconds before we're overrun," Jeff said, sounding as calm as could be, and Ben shot him a glare before Sparks shoved Ashley into him. He caught her with an *oof* and clutched her close as the officer fired her gun at the corner of a large pane of glass in the door.

"Come on!" Sparks kicked in the shattered glass, and then waved the others inside. She hopped in before Jeff and the four barreled down the hallway just as zombies started to squirm into the building.

"Stairs are at the back of the building!" Ben cried as he ran, holding Ashley's hand like their lives depended on it. They burst through a set of double doors and Jeff and Ben slam back against them to hold them shut against the pack of zombies behind them.

"It's the third floor," Ashley huffed.

"Go, make sure that key fucking works this time," Jeff instructed. "We'll hold them off until you give us the signal."

"When you come up, hug the right side of the wall," Sparks countered, and the guys nodded. As the girls took off up the stairs, the skinhead turned to the student.

"Bet you're really glad I'm a big badass motherfucker now, aren't you?" Jeff sneered, and Ben simply shook his head, grunting all of his energy into holding the door shut.

"We're clear up here!" Sparks called down the stairwell.

Jeff met Ben's gaze. "You ready?" he asked.

"After you," Ben replied.

"Alright, on three," Jeff said. "One. Two. Three!"

They both sprang off the door and hit the stairs, running up the right side as quickly as they could. The zombies fell all over each other as they staggered in the door, but quickly regained footing to pursue up to the first landing. They piled up towards the second floor but Sparks stood there, opening fire on them as they attempted to follow Ben and Jeff.

She struck the first zombie in the chest, the force causing it to slam back into the rest of the zombies, giving them a chance to gain ground. The hurtled up to the third floor and slammed through the double doors, slamming them shut behind them.

The zombies hit the doors, causing both Ben and Jeff to leap away from it. Ashley quickly ducked under Ben's arm and clicked the deadbolt, securing it.

"Okay, they're locked," the blonde said, chest heaving and heart pounding. "They aren't getting in. At least not through there."

"You okay?" Jeff clapped a hand on Ben's back.

The shorter man scowled. "Peachy."

"Where to?" Sparks asked, and the blonde pointed.

"Walkway is just through those doors. Building should be clear," she said.

Sparks reloaded her gun and cocked it with a *click* of finality. "Forgive me if I don't take your word for it."

CHAPTER SEVEN

Tuesday, 6:45 P.M.

Sparks led the group cautiously towards the lab, holding up a hand to stop the group at the sight of a pair of legs in the doorway. She readied her weapon and raised her chin.

"Jackson?" she called. "Michaels?"

"Sparks?" Jackson's voice from inside. "Is that you?"

"Yeah, I got the doc's assistants," she replied as he stepped into the doorway.

His eyes were wide and skin pale, and his gun was drawn but not in that normal arrogant way of his.

"What the fuck happened here?" Sparks demanded.

"My guess is the same thing that caused you to take five hours to run across the quad," Jackson retorted. "Get in here, we need to talk." He backed up and allowed them access to the room.

Sparks stepped over the body, which was one of the kids that had greeted them when they first arrived. He was missing the entire back of his head, shot clean off. Michaels' body was slumped against the far wall with a giant shard of glass sticking out of his neck, blood pooling beneath him.

The taller skinny kid tended to Agent Ross in the corner, who was missing a substantial chunk of his upper right arm.

"Let me guess, somebody got hungry?" Sparks asked.

"Deke here," Jackson began, kicking the body in the doorway for effect, "went into a serious coughing fit before collapsing to the ground. Michaels went over to check on him and next thing we knew, Deke pounces on him. Michaels lost his balance and went head first into an experiment, which is how he got the glass in his throat. Ross ran over and this asshole-" Jackson kicked the corpse again with a grunt. "-took a fucking chunk out of his arm. Just clamped down like a gator on an unattended child. Once that happened, I opened fire. Put two in his chest, but all that did was piss him off. So I put one right between his eyes, which calmed him down. Didn't see any other option."

"Yeah, headshots were the only thing that worked for us, too."

Sparks ran a hand through her hair with a sigh. "And Jackson, you did the right thing. Those things are vicious and there is no reasoning with them."

"Ms. Sparks is correct," Dr. Alvison spoke up as he walked out of the back room. He held a clipboard in his hands.

"Doc, you got anything for us?" Jackson asked.

"I think you all need to sit down," the old man replied, following his own advice as he lowered himself into his desk chair. "This is going to be difficult to hear."

Tuesday, 6:58 P.M.

Jeff and Ben deposited the corpses outside of the lab door and secured it, locking the deadbolt and making sure it wouldn't budge. Ted, the tall kid that had tended to Ross, drummed up chairs for everyone and they all sat in a crude semicircle around the doctor.

"I need to preface this by saying I've just started my research and everything I've found is preliminary," Dr. Alvison wheezed.

"Doc, just get to the fucking point," Jackson demanded.

"With that said," the doctor said with a huff, pointedly ignoring the rude strike leader, "what I'm about to tell you is accurate, although my timeline may be off by ten to twenty percent." He coughed and took a deep breath. "Okay. So, approximately eighty hours ago there was a bio-terrorist attack on the UT football game. A man infected with an unknown virus exposed roughly a hundred thousand people to it by wandering the grounds. I've determined that this virus is airborne, so everyone that attended that game was exposed.

"To complicate matters, it has a nearly one hundred percent infection rate, and once you are infected you become a carrier as well. I haven't been able to determine how long of a dormant period it has once someone is infected before they are contagious, but it doesn't appear to be too long. Maybe even as little as a few minutes."

"So what are you saying, doc?" Jackson cut in, furrowing his brow. "Are we all infected? Are we going to become those fucking flesh eating things?"

"To answer your first question," Dr. Alvison replied,

"yes, we are all infected. As to your second, it depends entirely on your blood type."

"Blood type?"

"Yes, Agent Jackson," the doctor confirmed. "Blood type. Whatever this virus is, it only becomes deadly if it infects someone with the A blood type. Something in the A blood type caused the virus to mutate, killing the host and reanimating it into the killing machine we witnessed a little while ago with Deke.

"I have been able to determine that for people with the A blood type, there is roughly a seventy-two hour incubation period before the mutation takes hold. Within twenty-four to forty-eight hours the person will develop flu-like symptoms."

"Like what you have?" Jackson asked.

"Yes, Agent Jackson." Dr. Alvison nodded. "Just like what I have."

A sob tore it's way out of Ted's throat and he turned away from the group to hide his tears in fear and embarrassment.

"And I'm guessing Ted over there as well," Jackson mused.

"Yeah," the young man stammered through his tears, "I have A blood type… but I'm not sick."

"You will be, son," Dr. Alvison said gently. "You just came into the office this morning, so it's possible you weren't exposed to it until you met up with Deke."

"So doc, lay it out for us," Jackson cut in. "How bad is it? How do we contain it?"

"The only way this could have been contained is if you'd nuked

Austin on Saturday morning," Dr. Alvison replied.

Jackson growled. "Don't give me that bullshit, doc."

"You don't understand." The doctor narrowed his tired eyes. "This virus is airborne, and it infects nearly every single person it comes into contact with. It has a hundred percent kill rate with people who have the A blood type, which is roughly forty percent of the population. As soon as the infected person left the stadium, this became impossible to contain."

Jackson turned and slammed a fist down onto the counter, knocking over a few beakers.

"Jackson, keep cool," Sparks snapped.

"I'm fucking cool, Sparks," he shot back. "I just don't like this defeatist attitude."

"The doc is right, though," she replied with a shrug. "Just stop and think about it for a moment. You have a hundred thousand people leaving the stadium that afternoon. Those people go downtown to 6th street for some music and infect tens of thousands more, including touring bands.

"They then take it on the road and infect more. Some people flew in for the game, including the opposing team. As soon as they hit the airport this virus goes global, especially if anybody they come into contact with has a connecting flight in a major international hub."

Her diatribe began to sink in, and Jackson's eyes seemed to glaze over with the severity of the situation.

"I've done some preliminary estimates on the spread of the virus." Dr. Alvison flicked through the pages on his clipboard. "Within ten days every major city in the world will have active cases of these creatures. If they are able to spread without the proper officials having knowledge we possess, I fear upwards of sixty percent of the population will either be those things or killed by those things within a month."

"What if the bites can infect someone who doesn't have A blood type?" Sparks wondered, and Ross stiffened, his free hand absently rising to clutch his wound.

"What do you mean?" the doctor asked.

"At the diner we saw two people who weren't showing signs of illness turn into those things after succumbing to their bites," Sparks explained. "I mean, it's possible that they both were A type and just hadn't been exposed yet, but one of them was the diner owner so it's unlikely."

"Assuming you are correct, the situation becomes much more dire." Dr. Alvison pursed his lips in thought. "Best guess? Seventy-five percent of the world's population will be dead within a month, and potentially as high as ninety percent here in the USA since we are at Ground Zero."

There was a somber silence, save for the sniffling as Ted's sobs started to mellow out.

"So, doc," Sparks finally broke the quiet, voice strained. "Realistically, what can we do?"

"If you can let your higher ups know the situation, they may be able to get the word out and some sort of quarantine effort may save some lives," the doctor replied.

"Well, given our immediate superior was worse than Deke when we left," Jackson cut in, "I'm going to go out on a limb and say that's not an option."

"Well, we're open to suggestions, Jackson," Sparks snapped.

"You know what?" He threw up his hands. "Y'all do what you want, but I'm getting the fuck out of here." He snatched one of the bags of gear and threw it over his shoulder.

"Oh yeah, and where are you going to go?" the redhead asked, crossing her arms. "Seeing as how you aren't familiar with the area, let me lay out your options. If you go North, you'll be in Austin, which is where this shitshow began. South isn't much better since it's San Antonio with one and a half million people. Now, you may be thinking east and trying to hit the coast. Assuming you survive the journey through the various backroads you'll be dealing with the population of Houston trying to escape this madness. So good luck finding a boat when a million people are all doing the same thing." She raised an eyebrow.

Jackson sneered. "Guess I'm going west, then."

"Great idea," she supplied, "except unfortunately for you it's all back roads. Take the wrong one and you'll be in a major city suburb. Now, I know a way to get us out, but we need to finish our mission first and get the word out about this."

"So, how are we getting out?" he conceded with a scowl.

"Canyon Lake is pretty close to here, and it connects right to the Guadalupe River," Sparks explained, turning to face the group. "One of the most popular spring break destinations is attached to it. You can get rafts to float, or you can get some boats if you want to explore. This thing is happening so quickly that I don't think the people here will be able to take all of them and escape. So if we get there, we'll have a good chance to jack a ride and escape via the river."

"And then what?" Jackson prompted.

"Haven't thought that far ahead," she admitted. "But it's sparsely populated once you get away from the lake. We'll be able to get away from all the major population areas and give us a chance to re-group from there."

"Well, I've heard worse plans," he said. "But what's your grand plan to get the word out? Everyone immediately above us is dead."

Jeff picked up the phone on the desk next to him and then slammed it back down. "And, anyway, the phone is dead."

"Yeah," Jackson confirmed. "So let's have it, Sparks. What's your plan?"

She shrugged. "We use the Hostile Zone Protocol."

"Great." He rolled his eyes. "So all we need is a functioning radio station, which I'm sure are plentiful in small towns this close to major cities."

"Well," Ashley said quietly, and then cleared her throat. "There is the campus radio station. Do you think that would work?" She wrung her hands in front of her. Sparks raised an eyebrow at Jackson to accentuate the question.

He sighed. "Goddammit."

"Ashley, where is the radio station?" Sparks asked gently.

"It's in the building across from this one on the top floor," the blonde replied. "Unfortunately there isn't a walkway so you'd have to go in through the ground floor."

"Which, if you've forgotten, isn't that easy of a task," Jeff put in.

"Then we do another distraction, only something a lot louder," Sparks said firmly. "I mean, we're going to need to do one anyway if we want any hope of reaching the SUV."

"What about firing some guns off of the second floor?" Ben suggested.

"No, our ammo is too precious." She shook her head, and let out a deep breath in thought. "And besides, we need something sustained."

"What about music?" Ted wiped furiously at his red eyes, finally having overcome his pity party. "I have this battery speaker set, you just put your phone in. The doc is always yelling at me to turn it down, so it's plenty loud."

"Alright," Sparks said with a nod. "Anyone got a phone with some loud music they don't mind parting with?"

"I got some R and B music on mine," Ben said with a shrug. "Not sure how loud that would be, though."

Jeff shook his head. "Lost mine back at the diner."

"I'm not giving up my phone." Jackson crossed his arms. "We may need the maps."

"Pretty sure mine is in the SUV." Sparks sighed.

Ashley put up her hand shyly. "I have some Slayer on mine."

Everyone gaped at her, and a blush crept up her cheeks.

"Goddamn, girl, you are a catch," Jeff said with an impressed grin. "If you ever decide to go back to vanilla."

"Motherfucker," Ben huffed. "Once you go black-"

"Yeah yeah." Jeff laughed, waving him off. "Don't worry, Chocolate Thunder, I'm just bustin' your balls."

Ben smirked, and the skinhead clapped him on the back in appreciation.

"Slayer it is," Sparks said, bringing the topic back on track.

"I'd suggest Raining Blood," Ashley instructed, holding out her phone. "It has a mellow thirty second intro before it kicks in, so you would have time to set it and run."

"Great, let's do it," the redhead agreed, nodding her head.

"Whoa, whoa," Jackson cut in, holding up his hands. "Wait a goddamn minute. I'm not going anywhere with anyone until I know who has what blood type. I'm not going to take a nap and wake up to one of you motherfuckers feasting on me. I'll start. I'm O positive."

Sparks pursed her lips. "O positive."

"B positive," Ben put in.

"O negative," Ashley added. They all turned to Jeff, who simply blinked.

"Do I look like the type of man who knows what kind of blood type he has?" he asked, raising an incredulous eyebrow.

"Ted, if you would, please test him," Dr Alvison motioned, and the student with the red-rimmed eyes scurried forward.

"Of course, doc," he said, and motioned for Jeff to hold out his hand. He pricked the bald man's finger and headed over to the corner machine.

"Ross, what do you want to do?" Jackson asked his team member in the meantime. "I can end it for you right now."

"Fuck that," Ross snapped. "I want to go out fighting."

"That's the spirit," Jackson said with a grin. "You want to kill some of those motherfuckers for us?"

Ross sneered. "Hell yeah."

"I don't mean to eavesdrop, gentlemen," Dr. Alvison piped up.

"What do you want, doc?" Jackson asked.

"Agent Ross." The doctor ignored the team leader and addressed his subordinate directly. "I know you want to exact some sort of revenge as your final act on this planet, but may I suggest another path?"

Ross shrugged. "Sure."

"I have a day left, maybe a little more before this virus over-takes me," Dr. Alvison continued. "In that time I plan on doing as much research as I can. Having you to study and do tests on could po-tentially help stem the tide of this pandemic."

"How you gonna get the info to them there, doc?" Jackson scoffed. "Carrier pigeon?"

"If Sparks is able to get a message out, I'm going to request she mention my research and where it will be," the doctor replied. "There is roof access to this building, so they can fly in and only have to deal with the three of us to re-trieve it."

"Ross, it's up to you." Jackson turned to his comrade. "If you want to go down fighting, I can use you. If you want to be a guinea pig that's your call."

Ross sighed deeply, lowering his gaze to the floor in thought. His lips twisted and he raised his eyes to the doctor.

"Do you really think I can do some good?" he asked quietly.

"I really do," Dr. Alvison replied with a nod. "And if it will help put your blood lust at ease, you have my permission to take me out when I turn. I'm sure Ted over there will appreciate it since he has an extra day or two before he goes."

Ross nodded. "Okay doc, I'll do it."

Jackson patted his subordinate on the shoulder as the doctor shuffled over to Sparks, who was speaking with Ted.

"I got the big fella's results," the student was saying. "O positive."

"Good to know," the redhead replied. "Thanks."

"Sparks, I have a request," Dr. Alvison cut in.

"Whatever you need, doc," she affirmed, turning to him.

"I'm going to write down some info about this building and my lab," he told her. "I need you to read it over the air so your people hear it. This information could potentially save millions of lives."

Sparks nodded. "Let me know when you got it, doc. Just hurry because we're on a tight schedule."

She turned to the group that had gathered behind her, her own post apocalyptic strike team. She took a deep breath. "So, this is our group then, huh? Alright." She looked to Ben. "I need a guide to take me to the radio station."

"I got that covered," he assured her.

"Jackson, can you three take care of the decoy and get to the SUV?" she asked, and he held up Ashley's phone.

"Yeah, we're parked just outside the Student Union so it shouldn't be that bad," he said.

"That's no good," Jeff spoke up with a shake of his head. "We had to open it up in order to get up here. God only knows how many zombies are running around there."

"Great, so how do we get to the car?" Jackson furrowed his brow.

"There's another walkway that goes into a dormitory," Ashley put in. "I have the key to the building and can guide you there."

"Good enough for me," Jackson agreed.

"Okay, here's the plan," Sparks instructed, commanding everyone's attention once again. "In twenty minutes that song needs to be blaring. Hopefully it will clear the path for me and Ben. You guys get to the SUV and get to a safe spot. When you hear me finish the radio broadcast come pick us up."

"What's the station?" Jackson asked.

"89.9," Ashley replied.

"We'll be there," he affirmed.

"You better be, since I'm the only one who knows where we're going." Sparks smiled, but she was only half-joking.

CHAPTER EIGHT

Tuesday, 7:32 P.M.

"That's a whole lot of mother-fuck right there," Jackson said quietly, taking a step back from the dormitory window.

Jeff shook his head. "Man, you ain't kidding," he agreed. He glanced at Ashley, who's face had gone deathly pale at the sight of the sixty or so zombies milling about in the quad. "You got any bright ideas?"

"Yeah, but you ain't gonna like it," Jackson replied.

"Seems to be the way today's going," Jeff huffed with a sigh. "Alright, let's hear it."

"Ashley, do you have a key to any of the second floor rooms?" The strike leader asked, and the blonde pursed her lips, taking in a deep ragged breath.

"No," she said. "They are all individual and only the RA has the master key."

"Don't worry about it," Jeff squeezed her shoulder reassuringly.

"You think you're strong enough to break down the door?" Jackson raised an eyebrow skeptically.

"No, but there's a reason I went to prison," the skinhead replied with a roll of his eyes. "A dorm room deadbolt isn't going to be much of a challenge."

"Fair enough." Jackson looked impressed. "You're a lot more useful than I thought you'd be."

Jeff barked a laugh. "I guess that qualifies as a compliment."

"Closest you are going to get from me," Jackson admitted. "Now look, I need you to go to the corner room and get the music going. Once you hit play you're going to have thirty seconds to haul ass to get out of the building and meet up with us."

"Man, you are out of your god-damn mind!" Jeff gaped. "This building is fucking huge. I mean that's gotta be what, an eighty yard run just for me to get to the stairs, then out the front door and over to the car? Maybe if I was twenty years younger."

"Alright, it's your ass." Jackson sneered. "What do you propose?"

"I'll have a good vantage point from up there," Jeff explained. "I'll hit the music, and keep up the distraction until I see you get to the SUV. As soon as you start the engine I'll kill the music and they'll start following you."

"Oh, *loving* this so far," Jackson snapped.

Jeff narrowed his eyes. "Yeah, well, unless you want to be the music man, you'd better."

"Fine, so I'm the pied piper, so then what?" the taller man muttered.

"You drive those things around the block," Jeff suggested. "You are going to be faster than they are, so when you make the return trip the entrance should be free and I can just hop in and we're on our way. I'll even restart the music just to keep them occupied."

"Works for me," Jackson sighed. "Ashley?"

"If all he's doing is hitting play and then waiting, wouldn't it make more sense for me to wait here?" the blonde asked, wringing her hands in front of her.

"Jackson and I can both handle ourselves against those things," Jeff said gently. "Unless you have some hidden ninja skills I'm not sure your ninety pound frame is well suited for hand to hand combat."

"Jeff's right," the other man agreed. "Stick with me, we'll be fine."

"Alright, let's do it," the skinhead announced.

"Maestro, the floor is yours," Jackson said, and held out the phone.

Jeff collected it along with the speakers, and headed upstairs. He took them two at a time and scurried down the hallway, keeping his senses on high alert even though it was unlikely there were any zombies around. He fiddled with the deadbolt for seventeen seconds before it gave, and he swung the door open to a bright pink room.

"Yikes," he muttered as he strode through the kitty cat themed room and opened the window. He positioned the speakers so they were pressed right up against the screen, clicked the phone into place and hit play.

As the intro to Raining Blood permeated the thick air, he sighed. "Well, at least if I'm going to die, I'm going to go out rockin'."

The zombies began to take notice of the noise as the crescendo built, and they sprinted as the song kicked into high gear. As they hit the wall in a vain attempt to get to the skinhead above them, he stood up and flipped them off, banging his head along with the crunchy riffs.

He stopped head banging in time to see Jackson and Ashley cautiously moving away from the door and break into a run for the car.

"Yeah, go get that big beautiful SUV," he said with a grin, but his smile faded as he noticed two zombies take off after them. With their trajectory, they would cross paths with his comrades before they made it to the car.

His breath caught in his throat as Jackson took notice, and then shoved Ashley hard, causing her to face plant into the asphalt.

"No!" he cried, frozen in place, heart pounding in his ears. "You goddamn motherfucker!" His mouth fell open in shock as he watched helplessly while the zombies descended on the poor blonde girl. He cranked the music up higher to drown out her screams, blinking in a daze at the sight of her flailing arms going limp.

Jackson, upon reaching the SUV, clicked the lights a few times to get Jeff's attention, and the skinhead's gaze darkened. He didn't want to give the bastard a reason to leave him behind too, so he cut the music.

The silence was deafening, and Jeff moved back from the window, ears ringing with the sudden quiet. He held his breath as the horde made a beeline for Jackson, who was revving the engine. He watched the SUV lead the zombies away, and then crept back to the window.

Jeff swallowed hard as he looked down at Ashley's body, splayed in the quad, half eaten, blood streaming everywhere from bite wounds.

"I don't know if you can hear this, girl, but I hope you can," he whispered. "You deserve at least that much."

As the song began anew, the gathering storm of the intro seemed to bring the blonde zombie back to life. She staggered to her feet, turning slowly with bloodshot eyes and a snapping mouth. And then when the intro led into a loud shredding guitar, she sprinted towards the building and growled, clawing upwards towards Jeff.

He looked around the dorm room frantically, and spotted a pair of dumbbells by the bed. He scooped up two twenty pounders, and returned to the window.

"I hope this finds you, girl, because nobody deserves to be cursed like this," he wished, and then punched out a screen, holding one of the bells out the window. He dropped it and watched as it plummeted directly onto her forehead.

She crumpled to the ground in a heap, and he nodded, cranking up the music to the maximum and running off to catch his ride.

CHAPTER NINE

Tuesday 7:59 P.M.

Ben and Sparks barreled through the door to the radio building, the student slamming back against it. He locked it with a click and tugged to make sure that it was secured, and then turned to the redhead. She raised her flashlight that rested over her drawn gun, sweeping the lobby cautiously in case the building wasn't clear.

"Don't worry, this building has been locked for a few days now," Ben assured her.

"Better safe than sorry," Sparks replied.

He nodded. "Fair enough."

She motioned for him to lead the way, and he jogged to the stairwell.

"Just a short walk up to the third floor and we're there," he said, trying to sound optimistic. In reality he was worried to death about Ashley. But he had to focus on the task at hand. He glanced over at the police officer, who was shaking her head in thought. "You okay?" he asked, brow furrowing.

"Yeah, I'm just thinking," Sparks mused. "I wish there was a way to get the information out to the people close to us. I know this message is for the Feds, but people here need to know what's happening."

Ben pursed his lips. "I might have an idea."

"I'm all ears," she replied, glancing at him expectantly as they hit the second floor landing.

"About six months ago, the radio station made a big push to get new listeners, so they ran some contest that required people to sign up to receive the occasional text message," he explained. "That way when some of the big shows on the station would have an important broadcast, people would get a text."

"I can't imagine there are a whole lot of people who signed up," Sparks said with a sigh. "I went here, and the radio station wasn't that good."

"Some is better than none though, right?" Ben asked.

She chuckled dryly. "Thanks for the optimism." They reached the third floor and entered the broadcast room. Ben secured the door once again, and then headed into the booth to check the computer. Sparks grabbed one of the notepads and a pen and jotted down a few bullet points for what she needed to say, as well as uncrumpling the paper Dr. Alvison had given her.

"Hey, Sparks, I found the message app," Ben called from the booth. "What do you want me to say?"

"Just say there is an emergency broadcast in two minutes," she replied, and at the sound of his fingers hitting keys, she took a few deep breaths. She muttered to herself, running over the way she wanted to give her speech.

Ben hit enter and poked his head out of the booth. "Are you ready?"

"Let's do it," Sparks replied with a firm nod. "Just be sure to record it so we can set it to repeat."

He set it up and started the broadcast as she entered the booth and took a seat. The LIVE button flickered on and she straightened her back.

"Hello everyone, this is an emergency broadcast, so if you can, please listen carefully," Sparks began, and cleared her throat. "My name is Lacy Sparks, and I'm an officer with the Austin Police Department. I have been working with Homeland Security under the direction of Special Agent Harris who was assigned to Austin.

"Three days ago, there was a bio-terrorist attack in Austin that sickened a lot of people, and has turned them into the zombies that you have no doubt encountered. We don't know a lot about the virus, but I will share what I know. It is airborne, and it targets everyone with an A blood type. If you or someone you know has A blood type, they need to be quarantined immediately. Do *not* try to get to the hospital or attempt treatment, as there is no cure.

"The virus turns the victim within seventy-two hours of infection, and is preceded by flu-like symptoms. Once someone turns, they will attack everyone in their vicinity by attempting to bite. If you are bitten, regardless of blood type, you will be infected too. If you encounter one of these creatures, do *not* attempt to communicate or reason with them. Either run away or destroy the brain.

"To the feds who are hopefully listening, you need to send someone to the Texas State University Campus and Dr. Alvison's lab. It's on the third floor of the science building. There is a treasure trove of research that will hopefully save lives there. The entry point is on the roof, however be ready when you enter the lab as Dr. Alvison and two others may be reanimated there and ready to attack.

"To any survivors in the San Marcos area who are listening." Sparks swallowed hard, and took another deep breath. "It's now eight o' seven PM on day zero. There are a small group of us who are going to attempt to escape via the Guadalupe River. We are leaving at the end of this broadcast and are headed to Canyon Lake. If anyone does make it out, we will leave a notice of where we stop on the river. It's rural and sparsely populated, which is our only real chance and survival.

"Once this thing fully hits Austin and San Antonio, there will be hundreds of thousands of those creatures running through the streets. If you are thinking of trying to ride this out, I implore you not to. There is no help coming. This virus will end everything. From this moment forward, for all intents and purposes, we are on our own. I know that's not an easy thing to hear, but it's our reality." Another beat, another deep breath. She looked to Ben, and he gave her a thumbs up and an encouraging smile. "This message will be left on repeat for as long as the station has power. Good luck," she finished, and nodded to him.

Ben switched off the live feed, and set the recording to repeat. After a few seconds, her message started again over the airwaves.

"How'd I do?" Sparks asked.

"You did well, Sparks," Ben said with another smile as he stood up. "You did well."

"Come on," she replied, and cocked her gun. "We hopefully have a ride to catch."

CHAPTER TEN

Tuesday, 8:06 P.M.

Jackson backed the SUV into an alley and killed the lights. He and Jeff held their breaths for a beat, straining their ears. There was no sign of any zombies following, having gone after Slayer to trample Ashley's body in an attempt to get to her phone in the window.

"I think we lost them," Jackson breathed, and then his vision exploded in fireworks as Jeff's fist connected with his face.

The skinhead went in for another lunge across the seat but the strike leader cocked his gun.

"Calm the fuck down there, cowboy," Jackson warned.

"You motherfucker," Jeff growled, "you just murdered that girl."

"That girl was fucking useless," Jackson snapped. "What good is a ninety pound waif going to do in this situation?"

"So, what," his reluctant partner replied, throwing his hands up. "You just going to kill everyone who isn't useful?"

"Well, it's the only reason I haven't pulled this trigger yet." Jackson sneered and leaned forward a touch. "You have skills I can use that will help me survive. That's all I care about. Now, are you going to shut up and keep being useful? Or do I have to end you right here and now?"

Jeff scowled, but lowered his hands. He turned in his seat to face

the front of the vehicle and let out
a deep sigh.

"That's a good doggy," Jackson
cooed. "Now, when we pick them up,
you don't say a goddamn thing. You
got it?" He slung his hand over the
wheel as his passenger nodded in de-
feat.

"*This message will be left on
repeat for as long as the station
has power,*" Spark's voice said over
the radio. "*Good luck.*"

"Sounds like they're done,"
Jackson said, starting the engine
and putting the SUV in drive. "Let's
go get them." He rounded the corner
but a few of the zombie stragglers
began following behind. "Shit, they
spotted us." He furrowed his brow in
thought.

"Remember asshole," Jeff spoke
up, breaking into his train of

thought. "I don't know the way to the escape point." The strike leader grimaced before punching the accelerator in the direction of the radio building.

Tuesday 8:10 P.M.

Ben had his hand resting on the deadbolt, ready to throw the door open at a moment's notice. There was a *honkhonk* in the distance and he furrowed his brow.

"That can't be good," he muttered.

Sparks cocked her gun. "Get ready to move." He unlocked the deadbolt and they both dropped their knees a bit to be ready to spring. As soon as the SUV rounded the corner, he threw open the door and the two darted outside.

Sparks grasped the handle as soon as the vehicle was within range, and flung the door open. Zombies hurtled towards them as Ben dove in and she leapt up after him.

"I'm in, go!" she screamed, and Jackson punched the accelerator.

"Where is Ashley?" Ben looked around the SUV maniacally, even looking over the backseat into the trunk. "Where the fuck is Ashley?!"

"She didn't make it, kid, now shut the fuck up and let me drive," Jackson replied, and the student launched himself into the front seat. Sparks lashed out and grabbed his shoulders, wrestling him back with her.

"It's okay," she whispered, and he struggled to steady his breathing, throwing her arms off of him.

"Sparks," Jackson prompted, "where the fuck am I going?"

"We gotta get on highway 308," she replied, keeping an eye on Ben as he leaned his head back, closing his eyes.

"That doesn't help me," Jackson warned.

Sparks turned to face front and her heart skipped a beat. "Turn left now!" She cried, and he skidded over the sidewalk, tires squealing. He slammed on the brakes at the sight of a zombie horde blocking the road.

"Ideas?" he drawled.

"This thing have four wheel drive?" Sparks pursed her lips.

Jackson raised an eyebrow. "Yeah." The zombies realized there was a meal on wheels in front of them and started to move towards the SUV, groaning and snapping.

"Hit the field, try and stay as close to true south west as you can," Sparks instructed.

"Good enough for me," Jackson agreed and hit the gas, turning to the left and directly into a chain link fence. The SUV tore through it like butter but the bumpy field was a lot slower than the vehicle's capabilities on pavement. "Not the swiftest of getaways." He glanced in the rearview mirror where the zombies were keeping pace with them.

"Just keep going straight," Sparks said, pulling up a map on her phone she'd retrieved from the floor. "In a couple of miles we should hit the road. When you do, hang a left." Jackson made a noise of affirmation, and Sparks turned to check on Ben.

"You okay?" she asked quietly.

"No, I'm not," he seethed. "Once we're out of danger, I'm going to find out what the fuck happened to her." He leaned forward. "You hear me?!"

Jeff clenched his fists in the front seat, biting down on the inside of his cheek to keep from saying anything.

CHAPTER ELEVEN

Tuesday 8:37 P.M.

"Clear," Jackson called from the back of the boat shop.

"Clear," Sparks called back, and the bell jingled as Jeff secured the door, standing watch. "Ben, get behind the counter and see if you can find some keys to the boats outside," she instructed. "Having a motor boat is going to get us a lot further than a canoe."

He nodded and headed to the counter, ducking down to check all of the shelves and drawers.

"We have survivors," Jeff called, and both the redhead and Jackson ran to the window, watching a young couple sprint to the pier. Two zombies emerged from behind a stack of canoes and made a beeline for them, but they continued trying to get to the boats.

The zombies tackled them and chowed down, the sounds of snapping and gurgling echoing off of the water.

"Motherfucker," Jackson muttered as the couple reanimated, effectively doubling the amount of enemies outside.

"Jackson, what's your ammo looking like?" Sparks asked as she checked her clip.

There was a series of clicks as he checked his own. "Mostly full mag, one in reserve, you?"

"On my last mag," she replied.

"Think we can get four headshots on moving targets in the dark?" Jackson asked wryly.

"Maybe with a scoped AR-15," Sparks scoffed. "Not liking the odds with a handgun."

"Well, whatever we're going to do, we'd better do it before the horde gets here," Jeff pointed out. "Four against four is a lot better than four against four hundred."

"Ben, you got keys?" Sparks asked.

"Yeah, not much else, though." He stood up from behind the counter, a handful of silver in his hand. "Just some knives. No guns."

Sparks nodded. "Grab the knives." She glanced over at a stack of wooden oars, picking up a few to inspect them. She brought one down over her knee, testing the strength.

"What, you want to beat them to death?" Jackson asked, skepticism in his voice.

"We're going to do a little teamwork," Sparks replied, slinging an oar over her shoulder, satisfied. "You guys are going to run ahead of us and use the oars to clothesline them. When they are on the ground, Ben and I will finish them off with the knives."

"You've got to be fucking kidding me." Jackson rolled his eyes.

She put a hand on her hip and shot him a level stare. "Well, we have a matter of minutes before we're overrun, so if you have a better idea, I'm all ears."

He contemplated for a moment before letting out a disgruntled sigh. "Give me the oar." He held out his hand and she plonked the length of wood into it.

Ben handed her a knife and they followed their oar-wielding team-mates outside.

"You ready?" Jackson held the impromptu weapon out in front of him.

Jeff grinned. "Whenever you're ready, sunshine.

Jackson let out a yell in response, grabbing the attention of the four zombies meandering around the pier. The living men sprinted towards them, holding their oars up, in perfect position as the zombies came at them.

Jeff's oar hit with tremendous force, sending both of his zombies flipping back onto the sandy ground. Jackson wasn't so lucky, his oar snapping in two with the first opponent. He slammed directly into the last one, tumbling them both to the ground.

Ben and Sparks darted in behind Jeff and stabbed his two in the face before they could scramble back up. Jackson's first managed to get halfway up before the skinhead swung and took its feet out, giving Sparks an opening to stab it in the temple.

Jackson cried out, on the bottom of a wrestling match with his opponent. He held the zombie's throat, twisting his head just out of reach of snapping teeth, and then got a grip on his broken oar. He shoved it directly through his attacker's head and kicked the body off of him as blood spewed everywhere.

"Yeah, thanks for the help there, asshole!" he snapped as he got to his feet, glaring at Jeff.

The skinhead shrugged. "Hey, I carried my weight."

Before a tussle broke out, the sound of shuffling feet and groaning wafted in from the distance, and the quartet glanced around at each other.

"Finish this later guys, we gotta go," Sparks barked, and ran towards the motorboat at the end of the pier. Ben stayed hot on her heels, and Jackson simply cocked his gun while staring Jeff down.

"You'd better watch yourself, boy," he said darkly and walked off towards the others.

Jeff stood motionless for a moment, deliberating.

Ben turned back when he realized he didn't hear the others coming, and his jaw dropped at the sight of Jeff smacking Jackson in the back of the head with his oar.

The strike leader hit the wood with a thud, fumbling his gun. It slid across the pier to the student's feet, and he took in a sharp breath. Sparks whipped around at the sound, drawing her own gun.

Jeff stepped over Jackson's groaning frame and picked up the gun, handing it to Ben.

"Jeff, what the hell are you doing?!" Sparks cried.

"The right thing," he replied, and put his hand on the young man's shoulder. "That motherfucker killed Ashley. Just pushed her into a couple of them so he could escape."

Jackson staggered to his feet and a ragged breath escaped Ben's throat. He raised the gun with a shaking hand, blinking back tears.

"I did what needed to be done so we could *all* survive," Jackson said, raising his hands as the horde noises grew in volume.

"Kill this asshole and let's go," Jeff prompted, and Ben aimed the gun. He clenched his jaw and then lowered it as the horde emerged from the tree line, closing in on them.

"I'm not going to kill him," Ben said, and the strike leader breathed a sigh of relief. But after the crack of a gunshot he clutched his exploded kneecap and hit the pier again. "But they will," Ben added in satisfaction.

"Goddamn that's cold blooded," Jeff said with a grin. "I like it."

"Come on, we gotta move!" Sparks screamed, untying the boat. Jeff and Ben raced over and hopped

in as she fired up the engine, pro-
pelling them out onto the water. The
guys watched with pride as the zombies overtook Jackson, his screams
quickly muffled by the thick pile of
rotting flesh on top of him.

"I'm so sorry man," Jeff said,
and patted Ben's shoulder. "I wasn't
close enough to her when it happened."

"It's okay, Jeff," the young
man replied. "I know you would have
saved her if you could." They turned
to Sparks, who hit the throttle to
speed the boat off into the dark-
ness.

They were out of immediate danger.

For now.

END